The Boy Who Got A Bernese Mountain Dog

Brook Ardon

CELLO PUBLISHING

LemonadeMoney ®

LemonadeMoney is a imprint and trademark of Cello Publishing Company Ltd, Hong Kong

♦ ♦ ♦

First published in the United States 7 December 2016
The Boy Who Got A Bernese Mountain Dog
Copyright ©Brook Ardon 2017
Adapted from the original 2014 (KDP)
Printed in the USA by Createspace, Inc, 2016
Brook Ardon asserts the moral right to be identified as the author
All rights reserved
Cello Publishing Company, Ltd (TM)
ISBN: 1539908445
ISBN 13: 9781539908449
Credit quote by Wayne Gretzky
Cover illustration by Crush Creative UK
Media email: contact@cellopublishing.com

♦ ♦ ♦

TO CARLOS

Savings Jar

I have decided to start this diary because I don't want to forget any of my teenage years. I have some exciting news—soon I might be getting my very own dog!

I was watching television when I saw a commercial for the postal service. It featured a huge Bernese mountain dog chasing the postman down a street. I knew right away that a Bernese mountain dog was the type of dog I would like to own some day. When I make my mind up about something I don't give in easily. I knew there was a chance my parents might allow me to get my very own dog.

I told my family, "I really want a dog! Please can I get a Bernese mountain dog?"

"I've never heard of a Bernese mountain dog. How did you find out about this breed of dog?" said Dad.

"I saw one on the television, and I think it would be perfect for me. A dog would fix everything."

Mom said, "Luke, a dog would be a whole lot of trouble!"

"I would be so happy if I had my own dog. I would never get bored if I had a dog," I answered.

"But a dog will cost money. How will you be able to afford to buy your own dog?" Mom asked.

"Don't worry about money. I will get a job and earn enough to afford a dog," I said.

"I don't care if you get a dog, but it will be your job to look after it. I'm too busy to help," said my older sister, Taylor.

"Getting a dog will be a big responsibility, Luke. Do you really think you will be able to manage it?" asked Dad.

"Yes! I'm ready for the responsibility of a dog." *Because how much trouble could a dog be?* I thought.

The following week I started my first job. I washed dishes at a local diner called Java Stop for three hours after school. Dirty dishes piled up, a mess of plates, saucers, cutlery, and oven trays. I spent my entire shift thinking about how amazing it would be when I finally got my very own dog, and I sped through the mountain of dishes.

The chef at work showed me how to make all different types of food when I got a break from doing the dishes. So far I have learned how to make all my favorites like: chocolate chip cookies, cheesecake, pizza, plus spaghetti and meatballs. I counted up all the money I had managed to save after one month of washing dishes. I put the dollar bills back in my glass savings jar and hid it back under my bed for safekeeping. I was disappointed because it had taken me one whole month to save just seventy-five dollars. I had a long way to go to save five hundred dollars. I calculated it was going to take too long just washing dishes, so I came up with a big idea for how I could save the money much faster. I told my friend Patrick about my plan and he agreed to help. We printed out flyers and placed them all around the neighborhood offering our lawn mowing service. I borrowed Dad's lawnmower for the job. Soon Patrick and I were busy mowing lawns and piling up bags of cut grass, sweating beneath the hot sun. Working together meant we could finish more lawns, and the more jobs we finished the faster the money piled up. All the time I was cutting grass, I thought about the adventures I might one day have with my dog. After just one weekend of mowing lawns, Patrick and I had managed to make three hundred dollars. We split the proceeds evenly then I counted up all my savings and I had close to half the amount of money I needed to be able to afford my own dog. I knew that in only a couple more weeks (not months), I would have all the money I needed.

After a few more weeks of work had passed, I brought my savings jar out from under my bed. It was filled with dollar bills, and I placed it on the breakfast table one morning.

"I have reached my savings goal—$500!" I announced with pride. "See, look in my savings jar. All the money is in here."

"Are you sure it all adds up?" Taylor asked.

"Yes, I am doubly sure. Because I counted it at least twice." I said.

"That's great, Luke. I'm impressed by all your hard work. You really sweated to save that money," said Dad.

"Yes, but it didn't really seem like work at the time. The work just flew by when I thought about getting a dog."

"You will be surprised by what you can achieve when you set a goal and work hard to reach it. We better start searching for that Bernese mountain dog now that you can afford to buy one," said Dad.

It turned out getting a Bernese mountain dog wasn't exactly as straightforward as anyone had thought.

Dad found a couple selling Bernese mountain dogs online; the only problem was they were located in a different country: Switzerland. After Dad talked with the couple over the phone, he gave me an update. The couple believed they had the perfect Bernese mountain dog for a twelve-year-old boy like me. But the dog was already two years old. The dog was called Benson. The owners had raised him since he was a puppy, and he had quickly become their favorite dog. They thought he had potential to become a show dog, so they had decided not to sell him until now. A new litter of puppies had arrived so they no longer had the space. They thought Benson would be perfect, because he has a good temperament, plus he would have to travel a long way by plane to get to us, and that would be a difficult journey for a puppy.

"So what do you think, Luke? Do you want to get this particular dog?" Dad asked.

"I don't know. I didn't think about getting a slightly older dog, but this dog sounds cool."

"It would be less work to get Benson than an untrained puppy. It would be difficult for you to look after a puppy when you have to go to school," said Dad.

"I need to think about it," I answered.

The more I thought about it, the more sense it made. I looked at the photograph of Benson that his owners had sent by email. The big dog was looking up at the camera with a wild look in his eyes, there was something that I recognized about this dog, it was exactly like the dog I had seen on the television. I knew I had found the right dog.

"I've thought about it and I think it's a good idea that I get Benson! Can we call the owners today and tell them?" I asked.

"We can give them a call," said Dad.

Soon Dad had already started making plans with the owners to transport the dog all the way from Switzerland on a jet. A dog is about to have his whole world turned upside down, and his new owner is just a twelve-year-old boy.

Special Dog Delivery

I had been counting down the days until my dog arrives, and today I finally got to meet my dog for the very first time. This morning Dad drove me to the international airport to pickup Benson. On the long drive I started having some doubts about my big idea of getting my very own dog. My stomach churned and I felt nauseous; maybe it was just carsickness, but I wondered: *What trouble was I getting myself into, getting my very own dog? Would my dog try to bite me? I hope my dog is friendly.* When we finally arrived at the airport I looked up at the sky and saw cotton candy–shaped clouds. I caught sight of a large jet aircraft descending at the very same time the sun broke through the clouds and cast golden rays down from above. I had a special feeling the jet I saw was carrying my Bernese mountain dog.

"Dad look, I think that's the jet bringing my dog from Switzerland," I said.

"It's a busy airport, Luke. Look at all those planes—it could be any one of them." He pointed to all the jet aircraft crisscrossed across the tarmac. There were jumbo jets with long wings and smaller planes with turboprop engines.

"No, I'm sure that's the right jet!" I declared.

Then the jet banked suddenly at a right angle and started descending quickly toward the runway. I heard the noise of the jet engines from the airport terminal where we waited. It was so loud, I worried about how scary an experience it must be for my dog spending so many dark hours traveling in a wooden crate in the back of a plane with the loud noise of jet engines.

I continued to watch as the jet landed smoothly. I saw passengers disembark down a tunnel that was connected to the jet at the terminal and then I saw workmen begin to unload cargo from the back of the jet. They unloaded a large wooden crate using a forklift.

"See, I bet that's the box with my dog inside."

"C'mon, Luke. We better go and ask at the airport desk. You might just be right. The plane is due about now," confirmed Dad.

The airport was busy. People rushed by hauling suitcases for foreign holidays, and business people were dressed in fancy suits and carrying briefcases. "Can we travel on a jet to go on holiday someday?" I asked Dad. But he was too busy looking at the large screens with different destinations and departure and arrival times flashing across the screen to hear my question.

"Which airline is Benson traveling on?" I asked.

"Let me double check the paperwork . . . Delta flight 801."

"Look, there it is on the board. It says that flight 801 has arrived!" I announced, with excitement.

"Okay, let's find somebody to help us find your dog," said Dad.

Next we found the right line for filing out the arrival paperwork so we could collect Benson, and joined a short queue. Dad handed me all the travel information for Benson, and then he walked off to buy a coffee from a newsstand.

I didn't have to wait long before the queue cleared and a lady behind the desk asked, "How can I help you, sir?"

"Hi, my name is Luke and I'm here to collect my Bernese mountain dog. He's travelling on flight 801 from Switzerland. Please, can you help me find him?" I asked.

"Okay, Luke. Can I see the paperwork?"

"Here it all is. I'm here with my Dad but he's getting a coffee," I said, as I handed over all the paperwork for Benson.

"I'm going to make a phone call. One minute . . ." said the lady from the airline.

"Sure, no problem," I responded.

"Good news—your dog has arrived, Luke, but he's waiting in the loading warehouse. He still has to have a medical check before we can release him, but I can arrange for someone to take you to meet your dog."

"Yes, that would be great. I would like to meet him right away. I've been waiting two months already!"

I followed a workman from the airline into the storage warehouse where my dog was being held. Dad followed behind us. I saw the wooden crate that I had seen earlier being loaded off the plane. It had the following words written on the side: "Attention: *Live Dog. Handle With Care!*" and *"Special Delivery. Origin: Switzerland."*

"Your dog is in there," said the workman.

I looked in a gap in the pine wood crate and saw two big, round, frightened eyes looking back at me.

"Hi, Benson. My name is Luke and I'm your new owner. It's really nice to finally meet you. I hope your flight wasn't too bad. First they have to do some checks to make sure you're okay," I explained. "How much longer do I have to wait until he's free to go?" I asked.

"I will bring him out to you once we've got the crate open and have done all the checks. Should be finished in about twenty minutes," said the workman.

It wasn't long before my dog was free and I caught sight of the workman walking a big Bernese mountain dog on a lead toward us as we waited outside the airport terminal.

My dog looked HUGE! The biggest dog I had ever seen in my entire life. He was striking with a long coat of tricolor hair, mostly jet black but white on his chest and brown markings on his head and paws. The dog had a big square-shaped head, droopy triangle-shaped ears, chestnut brown eyes. His front and back legs looked strong and built for the mountains, his paws were big like boxing gloves, and he had a long bushy black tail with a white tip. Hanging from his red collar was a silver dog bone–shaped tag with his name inscribed on it: BENSON.

"Look, there's my Bernese mountain dog!" I shouted.

"What a ginormous dog," responded Dad.

"Hey, Luke, good news: Benson has passed all the checks and he's free to go home with you now." The workman handed me the lead for my dog.

"Thanks! I can't believe how huge my dog is," I said. Benson was just as excited to meet me as I was to meet him. He had a friendly look in his eyes. He stood half as tall as me, and he whacked the side of my leg with his big tail with so much force it almost bowled me over. I could tell right away that all my doubts from earlier about getting my very own dog were unnecessary.

"Benson, let's go home and get your new life started," I spoke to my dog. Benson seemed to understand because he responded by pulling me on his lead toward the airport car park with so much power that I thought my arm was going to be pulled out of its socket just by holding on.

When we reached Dad's truck in the car park, Benson jumped into the backseat without any hesitation. I was surprised; he was so big that he took up the entire backseat when he lay down.

As we started the long drive home, Benson sat behind me, breathing down my neck, and drooling saliva all over the upholstery. Occasionally Benson leaned forward and stuck his huge head in the gap between the two front seats as if to ask, "Are we home yet?"

We stopped at a park along the way to stretch our legs and I gave Benson some water to drink. He must have been thirsty because he gulped the whole lot down in just seconds. Then we were back on the road for the final stretch. We arrived home late in the afternoon and the house was busy with my extended family visiting for the Christmas holidays. I was excited to introduce Benson to everyone and show him around, but he suddenly became very shy because all my visiting cousins were crowding around him trying to pet him all at once. He didn't like that so he took off running around the house in circles, dodging anyone who tried to get close to him. But the one person my dog didn't avoid was me.

"Don't worry, Benson. This is where you're going to live now. It's not usually so busy here. I know you're going to like living here as much as I do," I explained. He seemed to under-stand what I had told him because he calmed down after that.

We had only known each other for a few hours, but I could tell my dog trusted me. Benson and I had formed a fast friendship.

Obedience Class Fail

Tonight I took Benson to his first obedience class.

I had never thought about obedience training until a few weeks ago when Dad mentioned that I should take Benson to classes. I thought it sounded like a good idea, because I know Benson doesn't always understand me, and it could be dangerous if I can't communicate with my dog in some circumstances, like trying to cross a busy road.

In preparation for our first obedience class, I bought Benson a new red lead with a matching red collar. The obedience training classes took place at night on a field lit up by some yellow floodlights next to a small airfield. Night classes were more convenient because I was busy with school during the day. There were at least twenty-five dogs with their owners already on the field as Benson and I signed in for our first class. Benson was excited to see so many dogs all gathered together. He pulled me along on his lead as he went to greet every dog. He was too strong for me to hold him back. There were a whole lot of different dog breeds — Labrador, Alsatian, poodle, fox terrier — but Benson was by far the biggest dog in the class. Then we met our class instructor, a serious looking middle-aged woman.

"Hi, I'm Luke and this is Benson," I said as we shook hands. Benson was to busy sniffing another dog to take much notice of his new teacher.

"Nice to meet you, Luke. What a splendid big dog. Can I ask how old are you?" said the instructor.

"I'm almost a teenager!" I said.

"You will be the youngest student by a long way in this class. We're about to start. Take Benson over there and ask him to sit beside you. Good luck!" said our instructor, as she pointed toward the end of a line of dogs and owners all waiting patiently to begin.

The first command we had to learn was the most basic one: "Sit." Benson already knew how to sit on command so he had a head start over some of his classmates. I asked Benson to sit and he did it right away, attentively sitting beside me still on his lead.

"I suspected you might just be good at obedience," I said, as Benson looked up at me with a big grin. Benson already knew some basic commands when I got him, so he must have learnt some of them with his previous owner. But it wasn't long before we got stuck. The second command was much harder for Benson to master. We had to unclip our dog from the lead and ask him to stay. Some of Benson's classmates bolted right away across the open field, and their owners chased after them in pursuit. Our instructor shouted, "Bring your dog back here. Get your dog under control!"

Benson remained calm, sitting after I had unclipped his lead from his collar just like he was supposed to do, and I felt proud. I asked him to stay; as I started walking a pace away from him, Benson jumped forward from his sitting position to follow me.

"You're supposed to stay back there!" I tried to explain.

But Benson just looked at me with a blank expression as if to comment, "I don't understand this command!"

"We will try it again, but this time try not to follow me, okay?" I asked Benson.

But on the second attempt, Benson couldn't resist his anticipation of wanting to run alongside me as I walked away.

"You're supposed to wait back there," I said pointing in the direction from where he had jumped forward. I sighed. Benson made a high-pitched whine: "Hhhawwooouu!" He was getting frustrated too.

Our class instructor had been watching as I failed to get Benson to understand the command. She said, "It's hard to get your dog to understand you right away sometimes. But just remember to be patient, Luke. It's not easy for your dog to learn a new command at the start. I can tell Benson is smart so he will learn quickly if you give him time."

"I know he wants to do the right thing, but he just doesn't understand what I'm asking him to do. I thought it would be easier than this," I replied.

"Here's a tip that always works: find a treat Benson loves and then give him one treat right after he completes a command. Soon enough your dog will remember that he gets a treat if he does what you ask him to do."

"So I should just bribe my dog with treats?" I asked, surprised. I thought: *Maybe I'm not so different than my dog because my parents know I will do almost any household chore for a churro.*

"Yes, it works well with almost all the dogs I train. Don't forget to practice at home all the new commands so your dog doesn't forget what he has learned tonight."

Mom picked Benson and me up after our class had finished.

"How did it go?" asked Mom.

"It went okay, but we're both tired now," I said.

I had to squeeze into the backseat of Mom's wagon beside Benson, because Taylor was already in the front seat. She was still dressed in her gymnastics outfit. During the ride home I whispered to Benson, "I'm sorry I gave up so quickly on you tonight. I promise it's going to get easier for both of us." He raised his head and gave me a reassuring look.

Saxophone Struggle

I'm now officially a teenager!

I got a surprise when I looked in the mirror this morning, because I have acne on my forehead, and stubble is growing on my chin. Most of my friends have acne too so it's not that bad.

A few weeks ago I started my first saxophone lesson. During my first few classes I thought it was way too difficult. Learning how to read music is hard, and every score of music is different plus I kept forgetting where to place my fingers on the dials of the saxophone. It was a challenge to time my breathing right when I blew through the reed mouthpiece of my saxophone—otherwise I might have run out of breath and passed out!

Even my music teacher seemed dismayed by how bad I was after I showed no improvement after my first few lessons.

"I suck at playing the saxophone. Nothing I play sounds right. I want to quit," I complained.

"Luke, no one is any good at playing saxophone right at the start. You need to complete your homework. Are you practicing at home?" asked my music teacher.

"I try to practice, but I have been busy recently," I said.

The next week I decided to follow my teacher's advice and complete the homework I was supposed to do from the start. I started making a little progress, but nowhere near as fast as I thought I should be.

When I played my saxophone at home, I had a captive audience with Benson because I let him come into my bedroom while I practiced. He seemed to enjoy listening.

One afternoon while I was practicing, I got stuck playing a particular score of music. I quickly got frustrated. "Damn it," I said. Benson looked at me with a quizzical look, with his head tilted to one side as if to say, "It's not easy playing that saxophone, is it?"

"Now I know how you feel when you don't understand a new obedience command!" I told Benson.

If I played the saxophone correctly and the notes sounded like the smooth ones they're supposed to resemble, Benson would stretch his big paws out in front of him, wagging his tail as he watched me play behind melancholy, half-closed eyes. Compared to my saxophone teacher, Benson was an easy audience to please. At least to my dog I was a maestro like Mozart.

Dog Meets Beach

We moved away from the city right after my parents decided to separate (one year ago). My parents had bought separate beach houses in the same neighborhood, just one block apart. A minute's walk away from a sandy beach lined with green palm trees, and the translucent blue sea on my doorstep.

I preferred living here than living in city suburbia. There was always something to do; like surfing, snorkeling, kayaking and fishing. But moving between two houses every couple of weeks was annoying. At least my parents didn't fight anymore. My sister had to move between houses too, but ever since she met her boyfriend, Martin, she's usually hard to find. Benson was the only one who really understood what it was like for me; he followed me everywhere I went.

A Bernese mountain dog was supposed to live in the snowy Swiss Alps. I didn't know how my dog would adjust to beach life.

When I arrived home afterschool today, riding my skateboard the whole way, Benson waited for me at the gate. He was so excited to see me that he almost knocked me over as I walked up the driveway, jumping from side to side and barking. I rushed inside to drop my school bag in my bedroom. Then Benson and I headed straight down to play on the beach. Luckily the beach was a dog-friendly beach; he didn't have to stay on a lead the whole time.

Benson went really wild when we got down to the beach: he chased after seagulls, jumped up and down on the sand like it was a trampoline, rolled in the wet sand, sniffed the seaweed, dug holes, splashed through shallow rock pools, and chased another dog that just happened to be on the beach at the same time.

Next he picked up a long driftwood log with his mouth that had washed up on the beach. As he got a yard or two away from me, he'd suddenly change direction, and I had to jump out of the way so I didn't get sideswiped by the log, which he swung about like a baseball bat.

I tried to prize the log from Benson to play fetch, but Benson resisted, crouching down. He didn't want to let the log go. I could see his big white canines biting into the wood as I tried to wrestle the log free as Benson made a teasing grumbling noise.

"Grrrr...aaaa...hhhhhh!!!"

He didn't want to give up the log for anything. I could see in his playful eyes he knew I was playing a game with him. I didn't give up until I wrenched the log free from Benson's jaws. I tried to throw the log as far as possible and he sped after it like an F1 racecar. He pounced on the log as soon as it crashed back down onto the beach. Then he picked it up again, but as I tried to get close to him to throw the log a second time, Benson wouldn't let me get close. I guess he didn't like playing fetch.

When we returned home after playing on the beach, Benson decided to carry the log all the way back home. But there was a problem with his plan: the entrance to our front yard only has a narrow walkway. The long log in Benson's jaw got stuck against the edges of the brick wall on either side of the entranceway so that Benson was blocked from moving forward with the log still in his mouth.

I watched as he tried to figure out a solution for how to carry the log past the narrow entrance. First he tried to use his strength to push the log harder against the brick, but that didn't work because he only pushed up against his own force. Then he circled around and came back for a second attempt without changing anything about his approach from the first failed attempt. Finally Benson gave up his prize and dropped the log and followed me down the entranceway.

I thought: *Perhaps the reason why Benson liked to drag the logs he found on the beach was; Bernese mountain dogs were traditionally used as working dogs on Swiss farms, and for pulling milk carts from the farms down to the villages. Maybe Benson believes he's pulling a milk cart along when he dragged and carried those logs? Perhaps the work gave my dog purpose?*

The Surf Trip

I've been addicted to surfing ever since I started learning right after my family moved away from the city. I was lucky because I suddenly had a surf break right on my front doorstep. The wave broke both left and right so I could choose which way I wanted to surf any particular wave. I first started learning how to surf by watching the older kids in my new neighborhood. Some of them are really good surfers. They gave me advice out in the surf break like, "Paddle harder, Luke," and "Go for this wave". I found it hard to catch the right waves in the beginning, and to find my balance standing up on my surfboard, but then my surfing quickly improved.

During a good swell at our local surf break, Patrick would knock on my window and wake me up early in the morning before school. Then we would run over the road, down the beach, and paddle out into the curved waves turned gold by the sunrise. We practiced our maneuvers on our rides: cutback, re-entry, floater, aerials, and tube riding. With each wave ridden Patrick and I tried to out-surf one another. We yelled with excitement between waves at each other, "Did you see my aerial?" and "Did you see my barrel? I almost made it out!"

Usually when I go out surfing Benson always followed me down onto the beach and waited for me patiently until

I returned. If I caught a wave, he'd charge along the beach at the same time and direction that I surfed the wave. When Benson got tired of running along the beach, he stood in the shallows and barked at the waves washing up around him as if to ask, "Where do these waves come from? And why do these waves keep crashing into me? I don't understand . . ." But he didn't like to venture out very far into the sea, only a few yards at a time. Benson seemed to be afraid of the crashing waves, otherwise he probably would have swam out to join me out in the surf lineup.

If another surfer happened to walk down the beach to go out surfing, they had to watch out for my excited Bernese mountain dog racing to greet them.

Three weeks had flown by since Benson first arrived. I felt bad that I had to leave my dog behind already. I had to travel to a surf competition in a different city, and Benson would have to stay at home without me. I was worried about how he might react without having me around. So I told Benson just before I was ready to depart on my surf trip, "I have to leave you behind because I have to travel for a surf competition. It's really important I do well. You will be okay without me around for a week, right?" Benson looked worried as I placed my bag and surfboard inside the Winnebago my Dad had hired for our surf trip. Benson whined, "Wwaarroohhhh." As soon as we started driving down the road, Benson chased the Winnebago for three hundred yards. I watched my dog in the rearview mirror. He was running fast, taking giant leaps on his strong legs. I felt guilty about leaving my dog behind so soon.

"Do you think Benson will be okay while we're away? Look at him chasing us. I have never seen him run that fast before," I said.

"Don't worry about your dog. Your mother will take good care of him. Just remember how hard you have worked in preparation for the surf competition," said Dad.

"I just have this bad feeling that he might get into some kind of trouble while I'm away," I said.

I watched Benson eventually vanish behind us, unable to keep up. A few hours into our drive, Mom called Dad on his cellphone to say that Benson was missing! She couldn't find him anywhere and had been looking for at least an hour. Dad told me not to worry because sometimes dogs go wandering and return home later.

After we arrived at our destination where the surf competition was being held, Mom called a second time and said, "I've found Benson. He was hiding under the house and he's refusing to come back out."

"What should we do, Dad?" I asked, feeling worried.

"It's too late for us to turn around, Luke. The competition starts tomorrow. I think Benson is going to realize he's made a mistake and come back out in a few hours."

"I had a feeling all along my dog might do something stupid like this," I replied.

The following day, I surfed the surf break where the competition was being held. The waves were different from the waves I usually surfed at home and I wasn't feeling very con-fident. I struggled against the other surfers in my first heat. I tried my best and surfed a couple of average waves, but my concentration wasn't very good. I kept thinking about how Benson was doing back home hiding under the house. I lost in my first heat, which meant I failed to progress through to the next round of the surf competition. I was upset that I had lost right away after having traveled such a great distance for the com-petition, but I felt better when I realized that it also meant we could head home a few days earlier. I might be able to help my dog come out of hiding.

As soon as I arrived back home I ran up to Mom's house to find where Benson had crawled through a small gap be-neath the house. Mom came out and hugged me. She said, "Luke, I'm so glad you're back. I tried everything to get your dog to come back out from under there. He hasn't budged for anything."

"I'm sorry he caused you so much worry. I shouldn't have left him behind so soon," I said, then I called out, "Come out from under there, Benson. It's me, Luke. I'm back."

I looked toward the small gap beneath the house where my dog had disappeared and I saw Benson peering out from the darkness. Benson started moving slowly. Then he dragged himself on all fours, belly to the ground, and paw-by-paw he moved out from the small gap between two planks of wood, emerging into the afternoon daylight. Benson was covered from nose to tail with dirt. He started to shake him-self clean and dust flew everywhere. My dog greeted me with excitement and he forgot all about being afraid. I said, "What were you thinking? Hiding under the house for half a week . . . You had everyone worried sick. That was a really odd thing to do. I promise I won't leave you behind ever again," I said. But I wasn't sure I could always keep my promise to my dog.

Hiding From Fireworks

Last night the neighbors had set off booming fireworks without warning. The flashing neon colors of the fireworks brightened the night sky.

I went down to the front yard to check on Benson but he wasn't in his kennel. Instead he was tearing around the front yard with his tail between his legs. The whites of his eyes were glowing like light bulbs, and I thought: *He must be afraid of the loud fireworks*.

As I approached Benson on the front yard, we looked at one another for an instant before he decided to run down the driveway in a panic. He slowed down as he reached the gate, then he lowered himself beneath the gap between the bottom of the gate and the ground, crawling on all fours until he emerged on the other side. The next thing I knew he had disappeared into the darkness, and the uncertainties of the neighborhood.

I chased after my dog but I couldn't keep up or spot him anywhere. I searched the streetlight-illuminated front yards and empty driveways of the neighborhood. I called out, "Benson! Where have you gone? Come back here." But

Benson had vanished and I thought he might get completely lost.

After a few hours I had to return home and go to bed without finding Benson. I woke up early to a red dawn and from the porch, I caught sight of Benson walking up the driveway. I had left the gate open for him. He must have spent the entire night hiding from fireworks. I went down to greet him.

"I'm so pleased you're back. I could barely sleep because I was so worried about you being lost out in the suburb. Benson, why are you so terrified by loud noises? Is it because you were scared by the jet engines during your flight here?" I asked. He gave me a pitying look, which I read as him saying, "If only you understood how I feel about fireworks."

But I did understand. I didn't think he should be so afraid of fireworks because fireworks aren't as bad as Benson made them out to be. I decided to have a talk with Benson about his fear of fireworks. "I know fireworks can come at you fast, and then you get all spooked, but fireworks aren't that bad really. I promise." Benson raised his head and looked at me with his complete attention.

I continued: "I know what it feels like to be afraid of something. We're not that different, you know. We both have problems. I haven't told anyone this—it's kind of a secret—but I'm afraid of surfing big waves! So I know how you feel, but can you promise me not to run away next time you hear fireworks? It could be dangerous to run off like that again," I said. I didn't know if it was possible for a dog to understand what I was asking him to do, but I knew he had listened to me. In a strange way just talking with Benson about my fear of big waves felt like a weight had somehow been lifted off my shoulders. Perhaps I shouldn't be so afraid of surfing big waves.

Recently when a big swell hit the beach, I went out surfing with my friends and I didn't always catch the biggest waves (even though I could). Afterward, I imagined what it might have felt like to surf those big waves if I had found the courage.

I have a sticker on my bedroom door at Mom's house. With a picture of a basketball flying toward a hoop with the following words, "You miss 100% of the shots you don't take.*" I thought the quote meant that I should take more chances, otherwise I might miss out on something really awesome, and end up regretting it later.

* Credit: Wayne Gretzky.

Dog Graduate

Getting a dog has TOTALLY made me a more responsible teenager!

I try to be the best dog owner I can be, but between school, homework, and sports I don't always have as much time as I would like for my dog.

Practicing new obedience commands every week was not my only responsibility as a dog owner. I had to wash and brush my dog too. Benson always waited calmly while I brushed his loose hair free, but I had to chase after him with a hose if I tried to give him a shampoo wash. He grimaces and whines the whole time. He doesn't like being washed. I don't know why. I think most dogs don't like being washed though. A big dog like Benson eats a huge amount of food, and every week I have to carry the heavy forty-pound bags of dog food from the car up to the house. It felt like I was lifting weights at the gym. Doing all these jobs for my dog wasn't a problem—I was happy just to have my own dog.

Tonight Benson and I had our final obedience exam. I could tell Benson was excited as we arrived at the field next to the airport for our final class; he barked a couple of times. All the commands we had been learning over the last seven weeks were about to be tested, and my dog was going to have to pass the test to graduate from obedience school. I felt nervous as we waited in line for our turn, watching Benson's classmates perform before us. I was surprised to see that some of the dogs in our class hadn't improved very much at all. Some of the dogs misbehaved or just plain ignored their owner. I just hoped that my dog wouldn't forget everything he had learned when it came our turn to be examined.

When the instructor waved us over, I told Benson, "Remember how hard we've trained for this. I know you can do it." He was pulling on his lead, eager to get the exam started. Our instructor motioned to me that I should walk into the rectangle set with orange cones on the field. It was time to start.

"Luke, are you both ready to begin?" Our instructor asked.

"Yes, I think we're ready. Right, Benson?" He wagged his tail with enthusiasm, and then I asked him to complete the first command. "Sit," I said, and he responded right away, sitting at my side. We moved onto the next command. We both knew it wasn't going to be so easy. "Stay," I said. I crossed my fingers behind my back hoping that he wouldn't move as I walked five paces away. I looked directly at my dog so that I had his full attention. I could see he was resisting the urge to break from sitting and run alongside me. He understood what I had asked him to do, and he knew I had a treat in my pocket for him if he did it right. I counted my steps to five and stopped. "Come toward me," I called out. Benson hesitated. He must have misheard me. He looked at me, seriously not sure what to do, but as soon as I repeated the command he got it right away. Benson bounded dutifully forward right at me. I breathed a sigh of relief and sneaked him some dog treats as a reward.

For the remainder of the exam all I had to do was walk Benson around the obstacle course of marker cones. He stayed close by my side, just as I had taught him to do, without pulling ahead on his lead and with perfect timing. We both had a bounce in our step. Benson was a fast learner and he had picked up the more complex commands like heeling without any real problems.

I was proud of how well my dog had performed; all the commands that we had practiced over the last few months were completed without error.

Once all the dogs had completed the exam, our instructor handed us a certificate with Benson's name on it. It was a special moment for both of us. We had improved quickly since our first class and we could understand one another much better than before.

"Congratulations, Benson. You just graduated from obe-dience school!" I said proudly. Benson was happy; his tail wagged, and he looked up at me with a big grin, it was like he understood the achievement we had just accomplished. Then I let him off his lead to play with his classmates.

"Well done. Your dog really listens to you, Luke. Benson would make an excellent show dog. You should think about entering him into a dog show," said our class instructor.

"Thanks, we couldn't have graduated without your help. You were right about the treats working, and it's funny you mention it because his previous owners also thought he could become a show dog," I answered.

My family was also there to watch Benson and me sit our final exam.

"You both did so well," said Taylor.

"Good job, son. You never know when you might really need to use these commands with your dog," said Dad.

"You must be pleased with how well it went," said Mom.

"Benson really was the star tonight," I said.

When we got back home, I made Benson his favorite meal of spaghetti and meatballs, a special reward for doing so well at obedience school. "Thanks for making obedience classes so easy for me. I'm sorry I doubted you at the start," I said. Benson wolfed down his dinner. I knew he was listening because he looked up at me for a split second between mouthfuls as if to reply, "No problem. I had fun too!"

Climbing Getaway

I went camping with my friend Patrick to some rock climbing mountains.

"This particular climb is called Dead Dude," Patrick told me, standing in front of a steep rock wall.

"Did somebody die here?" I asked nervously.

"I don't think so, it's just to scare freshmen. It's an awesome name though isn't it?"

"I don't know about that," I answered.

I was starting to feel unsure about rock climbing.

"You see how the rock goes up in stages? That's where we climb." Patrick pointed in a zigzag motion at different rock ledges and points, only noticeable to somebody who was an advanced climber, not to a novice like me. Standing at the bottom before the hulking mass of rock, we were just tiny stick figures. I had a bad feeling about climbing up it.

Before we started the climb I decided not to tell Patrick that I didn't like heights. Looking up at the steep rock climb, I started to have some doubts about whether I could really climb to the top. But it was too late for me to just give up, and I didn't want Patrick to think I wasn't as bold as him.

We started unpacking all our gear for the climb: waist harnesses, climbing clips, climbing pegs, ropes, helmets, and climbing gloves. By 10:35AM we were finally ready to start our climb.

Patrick started rock climbing first. He had to hammer in some safety clips into the rock and let down a safety rope as a backup, just incase one of us lost our grip during the climb. Patrick was a confident climber. I watched as he quickly moved higher, without a seconds doubt, only pausing to think about where to place his hands and feet on the rock crevices so he could pull himself to the next position. I thought: *Rock climbing is like trying to solve a puzzle, but with real consequences if you make a mistake*. I started climbing and realized it was much harder than Patrick had made it look. About half way up I got stuck. I was trying to get over a rock with a steep angle sticking out, but the rock pushed into my chest as I tried to get over it. I couldn't get my arms far enough past the rock to pull myself any higher and my legs were starting to slip beneath me. Then I lost my footing and I was clinging to the rock with just my hands.

I gritted my teeth the effort of holding on was beginning to hurt, all the muscles in my arms started to strain just from holding on. Patrick was out of my reach above me. "Patrick, help! I can't hang on any longer," I cried, but it was too late.

I lost my hold of the rock and I fell backward. I looked up and saw luminous clouds against a blue sky. For a few seconds I felt weightless until the safety rope jerked and the harness tightened between my legs. I swung on the safety rope in midair. I looked down and saw nothing but the rocks at the bottom of the climb. I felt nauseous and giddy from the height.

Then, like a pendulum, the rope swung me back towards the rock face. I braced for the impact, I raised my arms in front of my head as I knocked against the rock face, I felt an instant jab of pain on my elbows and legs as they connected with the rock.

"Luke, here. Grab my hand!" Patrick called out from above me.

I reached up and grabbed Patrick's extended hand from above, and he pulled me up over the pointy ledge from where I had slipped just a minute earlier. Then we clambered up the final few yards to reach the top.

"Are you hurt?" Patrick asked.

"I don't think so, I just have a few cuts on my knees and elbows." I pointed to a few grazes where I was bleeding a little bit. "I just couldn't hang on that long."

"That was a close call. Are you sure you didn't break anything?"

As I got to my feet, I said, "No, I'm actually okay. I didn't want to tell you this, but I kind of have a problem with heights, that make me feel sick."

"You should have told me earlier, before we started the climb," he said.

"I know but I was embarrassed about it. I didn't want you to think that I wasn't brave enough to climb." I said with a sigh.

From the top the view was sweet. The pine trees below looked like tiny Lego pieces, the river glistened silver as it bent around the valley, and on the horizon we could make out the dark outline of the distant city. Patrick yelled out over the canyon below, "I'm the best climber in the world!" His voice echoed against the canyon.

"It's good to appreciate this view up here. Everything looks smaller, and makes you think differently about everything, doesn't it?" I remarked.

"I guess so, but we're not that high compared to how high some people climb. Hey, we should climb Mount Everest one day!" said Patrick.

"I don't know about that. But we could climb Mount Kilimanjaro instead, it's not as high, or dangerous." I said.

We ate our lunch admiring the spectacular view from above, a pair of eagles soaring above us.

"Thanks for saving me down on the climb. I thought for a second my life was going to be over."

"The safety rope is what really saved you. That's why it's so important to plan the climb in advance, even the best climbers can make mistakes," explained Patrick.

"I'm glad we came up here though, the view was totally worth the risk . . . Patrick, after my dog, you're my best friend!" I said.

"Come on, we still have to abseil all the way back down."

I was sick with nerves again just from the thought of abseiling down the rock face.

Shoe Thief

On the weekend, Mom came into my room and said, "Luke, one of my new shoes is missing from the backdoor. Who would steal just one shoe?"

She frowned at me as she spoke as if she suspected I had something to do with her missing shoe. I knew the shoes she was asking about. They were expensive Italian, blue leisure shoes. When I heard only one was missing I had a bad feeling because I suspected right away who might be responsible.

"No, I haven't seen your missing shoe, but I will keep a look out for it. I'm sure it will turn up," I said.

I went searching for Benson right away. I spotted him running back toward the house from the beach. I picked up the remaining leather shoe from the backdoor and walked to greet Benson as he ran up the driveway.

"What are you doing with my shoe?" yelled Mom. She had seen me pick it up.

"Don't worry. I have a plan to find your missing shoe. If it works I will bring the pair back," I replied.

Benson saw the shoe in my hand. In a second Benson snatched the shoe from my hand and started running toward the beach again. He had done exactly what I had anticipated he might do and my plan was set into motion.

I had trouble keeping up, Benson ran so fast along the beach. I didn't want him to know I was following him, so I followed behind at a distance. He ran toward the sand dunes at the other end of the beach. I was almost out of breath as I climbed over the sand dune; just in time to see exactly where Benson had gone, I was surprised by what I found. It looked as though a tornado had hit the area. It was like some powerful force had swept through and torn to shreds all the missing household items. I saw Mom's missing shoe, my sister's missing dress torn to shreds, socks, underwear, T-shirts, Dad's missing tool belt torn apart. I caught sight of my favorite baseball glove completely shredded. There were also piles of woodchips piled up like pyramids, with flattened areas of tussock grass were Benson had spent hours lying and chewing up logs.

Benson stood in the middle of all the household items torn to bits amongst the sand dunes. I had caught my dog red-handed because he still had one of the shoes still in his mouth, and the second shoe was close by. Benson looked surprised to see me, he mustn't have noticed in his excitement that I had followed him all this way to his secret hideout. I yelled, "Drop the shoe. Game over!" He dropped the shoe he was carrying in his mouth, in his expression I could tell he wanted to say, "Oh no, I never thought you would find out about this."

Sherlock Holmes would have been proud of my detective work. Although I never suspected before that Benson was responsible for all the other missing household items I had found alongside the shoes.

"You can't steal from your own family, Benson! If the rest of our family find out about what you have done to all their missing items, you will be in big trouble. I won't tell them on one condition: You must stop stealing right away," I told my dog.

Benson looked disappointed, he understood that he couldn't continue chewing household items to shreds anymore. I rescued my Mom's two expensive leather shoes from the sand dune. The only damage was a few indents from Benson's canines on the leather. As we walked back home along the beach together, I carried the leather shoes to give back to Mom, Benson trailed behind me at a distance of a few paces with his head hung low, and his tail between his legs. My dog sulked like a grounded teenager.

Summer at the Lake

We always spend summer vacation at the lake house. My grand-parents built the lake house many years ago after they made a fortune owning a textile factory. It's a big old log cabin with plen-ty of bedrooms for all our extended family; the log cabin looked out over an emerald green lake. There's a private beach with a jetty that stretches out over the lake, for parking the motorboat. The only way to reach the log cabin was by motorboat because the only road was on the far side of the lake where there are a general store and a single restaurant. My grandfather built the wood motorboat (named Javelin) in his garage from a kit set de-sign. It looked just like a motorboat from an original James Bond movie.

Benson was afraid of diving into the lake. He was a dog full of doubts as he stood on the end of the jetty, not sure whether he should follow my cousins and me as we dove into the cool depths of the water to escape the summer sun.

"Just jump in, Benson!" I yelled.

But Benson just barked and whined without having the courage to dive into the lake.

I found a way of getting Benson to dive into the lake — I ran really fast down the jetty and encouraged Benson to run along side me. Then, as I reached the end of the jetty, I dove into the water. Benson didn't have enough room to slow down and stop himself. Reluctantly he flew into the lake behind me, he was really bad at swimming. He moved one paw while his hindquarter sank. He barely managed to keep his head above water. He raised his right paw up and down, splashing the surface of the lake like a opera conductor. I thought: *aren't dogs supposed to know how to swim*.

When Benson managed to swim back to the lakeshore. He quickly got revenge for being left alone in the lake by shaking himself dry, sending water and sand flying all over us as we tried to sunbathe. I'm surprised that Benson didn't get any better at swimming despite this daily routine of us all jumping into the lake.

One evening I brought Benson along trout fishing for company. I'm allowed to drive the motorboat and sometimes I liked the solitude of just being out on the open lake as the orange light of the day faded away. I idled the two mercury forty-five mph engines, sputtering at their lowest speed, and set up two trout fishing rods with metal-painted lures to drag behind the boat to attract the trout. Benson lay at the back of the boat right beside the engines as we cruised past the small coves on the edges of the lake. I drove the boat past the other lake houses dotted in the different bays. The noisy Jet Skis that usually raced around the lake in the day were gone, and nothing seemed to break the serenity.

"This is pretty good isn't it Benson?" I said. Benson raised his eyebrows, and let out a loud sigh, in agreement.

Next I turned the boat around and headed back because it was starting to get dark, one of the rods started wheeling and bending. Benson got an awful fright and started barking as I darted over and picked up the rod next to where he lay.

"Calm down, Benson. This is the reason we're out here —to catch a trout," I said, as I reeled the line in. Benson was unsettled by what was happening; and he was getting in my way as I strained with the trout on the other end of the line. After a minute of reeling, I spotted the white and brown flash of the trout in the green water beneath the surface. As I pulled the trout right beside the boat, I reached down to grab the net to scoop the trout out of the lake and into the motorboat. Benson was standing on the net and his paw was stuck. While I took my attention off the trout and got the net free away from Benson, then the trout got off the hook.

During the first week of my stay at the lake house this summer, I went to a campfire party with a group of teenagers who were also staying in different houses around the lake. We grilled sausages and toasted marshmallows and talked around a fire. That's how I met Charlotte. We were sitting opposite one another. The flames lit up her beautiful face, and we made eye contact for a fleeting second. I knew that I had to be bold and go over and introduce myself. I had to make the first move to get to know this mysterious girl. If I didn't, I knew that I would regret it later. My heart was pumping so fast. I stood up and walked around to introduce myself, I accidently kicked some-one's drink over.

"Hey! Watch my drink, dude!"

"Sorry, man," I replied.

I sat down next to the pretty girl.

"Hey, I'm Luke! It's a pleasure to meet you," I said with a broad smile, but I mumbled my words because I was so nervous.

"Charlotte," she said simply, as she extended her hand.

We talked about all the normal stuff, like where we are from, and what we have been doing over summer break. Charlotte told me, she had only come to the lake because of her girlfriend's invitation to stay with her family; she lived on the other side of the country. While we talked I realized how much I really liked her, but I wasn't sure if she liked me in the same way.

"Let's walk home, Charlotte. It's getting late," her girlfriend said, and the two girls at the party got up to leave.

"Goodnight, Luke. It was nice talking. Maybe I'll see you around the lake," Charlotte said.

"Goodnight," then I quickly added, "Why don't you come sailing with me tomorrow?"

Charlotte looked at her friend and they both giggled. "Are you asking me out on a date?" asked Charlotte.

"Yeah! How about a sailing date?"

"OK, it sounds like a romantic thing to do," she replied before vanishing into the night.

"Meet me at the jetty at eleven a.m.," I yelled out.

"That girl really likes you, Luke," one of the boys around the fire said.

"You really think so?" I asked.

"Totally, dude."

The following afternoon the wind was howling like a hurricane and the lake was rippled with whitecaps. It was too rough for sailing on a first date so Charlotte and I lounged around on the edge of the jetty.

"You seem shy around girls! Have you been on many dates before?" Charlotte asked.

"Sorry, I get nervous sometimes. Honestly, you're the first girl I really like," I said. Even though I had been on a few dates before this one.

"I think you're handsome."

"I think you're really pretty."

I spoke so quickly we talked over one another. I reached out to hold her hand, and then we sat with our fingers intertwined and our legs brushing against one another, dipping our toes into the cool water, as fast-moving clouds made dark shadows over the shimmering surface of the lake.

"Everything looks so perfect," Charlotte said.

"It's nice here isn't it," I said.

We leaned closer toward one another she placed her fingers on the back of my neck, and my whole body tingled as we kissed. Nothing could ruin this sublime moment. I opened my eyes and looked past Charlotte. I could see something moving fast toward us from behind. The outline of the shape was blurry. I could make out it was black, white and brown.

Somebody must have untied Benson because I had purposefully tied him up by the lake house earlier so I would have no interruptions during my date. Benson came charging toward us at full speed along the jetty.

"Charlotte, are you wearing a swimsuit? Because we need to jump in the lake right now!" I said,

"Yeah, Ok, why?" We both quickly threw off our T-shirts. Charlotte was wearing a white swimsuit.

"Because my giant Bernese mountain dog is about to crash into us. Come on!" I yelled.

Charlotte dived off the edge of the jetty first and it was the most perfect dive. I watched as she disappeared into the lake almost without a splash.

Benson had almost reached the end of the jetty, so I cannonballed into the lake behind her. I popped up next to Charlotte just in time to witness Benson hurtle off the end of the jetty toward us. Benson momentarily blocked out the sun as he flew off. It looked as though he was going to land right on top of us and then Charlotte screamed.

Gravity intercepted, and Benson plunged underwater just missing hitting us, water splashed up like a giant geyser.

"Watch out for Benson. He's a terrible swimmer and if you get too close he will scratch you, with his nails" I warned Charlotte. Now all three of us were in the lake. Charlotte and I splashed water on each other and laughed while Benson swam towards us and in circles, before we all headed for the lakeshore.

"Sorry about Benson. I usually play a game of chase with him on the jetty so I can encourage him into the lake. He's actually afraid of the deep water," I said.

"I didn't mind. It was nice to go for a swim," replied Charlotte.

I found it easy to talk with Charlotte about anything.

Charlotte works part time as a barista after school, and her family runs a big farm with horses. Towards the end of our date I said,

"Can I ask you out on a second date?"

"Sure," Charlotte said breezily.

"I want to teach you how to wakeboard, tomorrow."

"I don't know how to wakeboard, but I will give it a try, I guess."

"Don't worry, it's really easy I promise." I said.

By the end of our date the sun was beginning to set and Charlotte had to rush off for dinner with her friend's family, the hours had flown by without us even noticing how late it was.

The next day, Charlotte was hanging onto the ski rope behind the bubbling and gurgling engines in the depths of the lake. Her feet were strapped into the wakeboard, her hair was floating around her and the life jacket she wore was keeping her head above the surface.

"When you feel the engines pulling you up, point the board toward the back of the boat with your weight on your back leg. Then let the power of the boat pull you up out of the water," I yelled out to Charlotte.

"OK, I'm ready." She replied.

Dad was driving the boat, and he hit the throttle to high speed. Charlotte was still submerged under the water, and she let go of the ski rope, unable to ride to the surface.

"Stop, Dad, she's let go," I told him, and my dad circled the boat around for another attempt.

"Are you okay?" I asked. Charlotte was spitting out water as we circled past her.

"Yes, although I swallowed a few pints of the lake."

"This time try to hold on a little longer. Once the boat gets faster you should be able to raise to your feet easily enough," I instructed.

"OK, I'll try again."

The second attempt was another fail. Benson was also in the boat and, seeing Charlotte fall again, he let out a loud bark.

"You're getting close. This time we will try a little a slower start. Just trust me and hang on," I said. "Dad, this time can you try going slower on the throttle?"

"OK, Luke."

"You can do it, Charlotte. Just hang on longer this time!"

"I'm ready. Go!" Charlotte yelled. She disappeared below the surface but this time she held onto the ski rope.

"Faster now, Dad!" I shouted over the growing roar of the whining engines. Charlotte rose up out from the turbulent bubbling water to stand on the surface. She rode the wakeboard as the boat turned and pushed her from one side to the other over the rising walls of the wake. We smiled at one another as she swung behind the boat standing on the wakeboard. Then after a few minutes, she fell off.

"Grab my hand," I said to Charlotte after she handed me the wakeboard from the lake.

"That was so much fun! Thanks for teaching me how to wakeboard, Luke." Charlotte said, as I pulled her up into the boat.

"You're a natural wake boarder," I told her, and she blushed.

I threw the wakeboard into the lake and dove in after it for my turn. Benson was barking the whole time as I jumped from one side of the wake to the other on the wakeboard. As much as I tried I couldn't take my eyes off the beautiful girl watching me from the back of the boat. I wanted to show Charlotte all the tricks I knew how to do on the wakeboard, then I decided to try and show her the one trick I had never been able to accomplish before—a backflip.

I leaned further out away from the boat so that the ski rope pulled tight like a slingshot. I turned on my heel so that the wakeboard aimed back toward the wake. I knew I had to time my launch from the wake perfectly and as I got closer I bent my knees, crouching as low as I could so I could spring into the back flip. I launched with the wakeboard pointing up toward the sky. I leaned backward in the air so that I tipped backward. I tucked my knees close to my chest as I pivoted upside down with the wakeboard above my head. Then, just as I had rolled up like a ball into the flip, I rolled back out as I came down for the landing on the other side of the wake, my body extended as I landed perfectly. I had done the one trick I never thought I would be able to land, and it seemed so easy when I finally landed it.

The rest of our summer vacation together flew by. Each day we grew closer, and I felt more comfortable spending time with a girl, but each day we knew was one day closer to being pulled apart by the end of our vacation. We spent the remaining week doing plenty of fun lake activities together: swimming, sunbathing, sailing, kayaking, and rock jumping.

On our last night together before Charlotte had to leave for home we sat together in front of a campfire on the lakeshore just like we had the first night we met but tonight. We both knew we only had a short time together. We sat close to each other with the Milky Way shining above; a crescent-shaped moon beamed back at us.

"I don't want you to leave," I said.

"I don't want to go home either," Charlotte said.

"Will you remember me when I'm gone?"

"Yes, of course, Luke."

Suddenly a dazzlingly bright, fiery, yellow-gold ball of light darted across the black night sky, it broke apart into small pieces before it vanished completely, the trajectory arched somewhere over the horizon. The meteorite had vanished all within less than a second, burning up in the atmosphere. We were both surprised by its beauty and our luck at being able to witness such an amazing spectacle.

"Meteorite!" I exclaimed.

"I thought it was going to crash right on top of us," Charlotte said. "I thought the same thing, but they look closer than they really are. It's kind of an illusion."

"That was so spectacular," remarked Charlotte.

"Yes. Did you know they've proven Einstein's last unproven theory. Gravitational waves actually exist in space," I said.

"No I didn't hear about that. That's cool."

"Hey, we should make a wish! After all how lucky are we to see a meteorite so close."

"Tell me what you wished for?" Charlotte asked.

"I don't want to tell you, otherwise it won't come true."

The next day, I walked around to Charlotte's friend's place as they were getting ready to leave. I gave Charlotte a hug and I didn't want to let her go.

"Don't forget our meteorite," I said.

"How could I ever forget?" Charlotte said smiling.

"Me or the meteorite?" I asked.

"I won't forget either."

"So I guess this is goodbye then. It's a pity we live so far apart."

"Yes, it's a shame, but maybe we can still talk sometimes on the phone?" She asked.

Charlotte was late and had to go, I watched as she climbed into her friend's car.

"Bye, Luke!" She called out.

"Goodbye, Charlotte!"

As the car began to pull away, she leaned out the window blew me a kiss and yelled, "I love you, Luke."

My first summer romance ended as quickly as it had started. I watched the car drive away, and I realized we had forgotten to exchange numbers.

Falling in love for the first time was totally bittersweet!

Stardog

I decided to enter Benson into a dog show. I found the advertisement for the dog show competition in the local newspaper. I remembered what my obedience instructor had told me so I entered Benson into the big dog category. I always had a feeling my dog was destined to be a star and I wanted to give him the opportunity.

At the start, Benson and I watched the other dogs perform from the sidelines. There was a giant Great Dane (the only dog I'd ever seen bigger than Benson); and a mixture of other big dog breeds in the hall, from a Golden Retriever to an Alsatian. Benson was the only Bernese mountain dog entered in the competition.

I knew any small mistakes during our routine would impact our score, I said, "Don't get distracted by all these dogs and pay no attention to the big audience. When it's our turn on stage just stay focused on me, okay?" Benson looked confidently back at me. I had a knot in my stomach because I was nervous about going onstage. I had to forget about my nerves. It was Benson's big chance to be a star and I didn't want to be the one holding him back.

Before the dog show started, I had to brush Benson's long coat of hair, and then he looked really smart. Because I knew the judges gave marks out for grooming and appearance and not just obedience. I also tried to look smart; I wore a tidy black sports jacket, a blue tie, a white shirt, and black jeans with black shoes.

Benson and I walked out. My dog walked closely by my side just like he was supposed to do. The lights on the stage made me squint, I said, "Are you ready, Benson?" He responded by attentively looking up at me as if to say, "Yes, let's get this party started."

Commands that were once a struggle for us to learn we easily did, like *stay* and *wait* and *fetch*. Nothing was forgotten from obedience school. After successfully showing everyone in the hall how good my dog was at basic obedience, we moved onto the harder part of the routine.

"Lift your paw up," I asked, and Benson raised his right paw. "Now wave, Benson," I said, and he waved his right paw just the way I had taught him to do. "Nice work."

We reached the final trick, the cherry on the sundae, but the toughest one of them all.

"Spin around," I asked, and he spun around in a fast 360-degree turn, it looked as though he was chasing his tail. He stopped exactly at the same point from where he had started out. I smiled at him. "You did it! Well done, boy!" I petted him for a few congratulatory seconds. I turned to face the judges and audience. I bowed, and then we both walked off stage. From start to finish our whole routine lasted only a few fast minutes.

During the prize-giving ceremony, the head judge announced the results. "The winner of the large dog category is contestant number eight: a Bernese mountain dog. Congratulations Benson and to his teenage owner, Luke Fine."

I could hardly believe my ears, hearing that we had actually won, and it seemed like a dream. Benson got a blue ribbon placed over his head by the head judge, and then she handed me the first-place prize: a check for five hundred dollars. I thought: *In a funny way Benson had paid me back the money I first saved to buy him.* I planned to transfer the check into my savings account.

Next we had our photograph taken by a photographer from the local newspaper.

"Wow, Benson you won," I told him. Benson beamed with a big grin and seemed to enjoy all of the praise he had worked so hard to achieve.

Sister Trouble

I doubt I will ever be as COOL as my sister!

Taylor came into my room and told me her plan. She said, "I'm leaving with Martin. There's a music festival with my favorite punk rock band. I can't miss going for anything. But you can't tell our parents. I wanted to tell you, I can trust you to keep it a secret, can't I, Luke?"

"How are you going to travel all that way to the music festival? You will get grounded forever when our parents find out about this,"

"Martin is going to borrow a car and drive us. I just really wanna go. When you're older you will want to do the same thing."

"Martin isn't exactly a reliable guy. Do you really trust him to look after you? What if you get into some kind of trouble?" I asked. I knew Martin didn't have the best reputation for being responsible.

"You don't know what it's like to be in love. I love Martin, and he loves me back, I know he's going to look after me. "

"I don't think it's a good idea, that's what I think."

"Just promise me you won't tell our parents?"

"Okay, I promise." I said.

Benson had been listening in on our conversation, and he looked worried about Taylor too. I said, "We can't do anything to stop her, Benson. Taylor isn't going to listen to me and she always finds a way to do whatever she wants."

I was surprised that she had decided to confide in me, but we trusted one another. But I also felt a sense of dread about what she was planning, because I knew I was responsible by keeping it a secret.

The following day Taylor had already left town. Mom was worried and she asked me if I had seen my sister.

"No, Mom. She's probably just staying with a friend, you know what she's like always sleeping over somewhere," I lied. I felt guilty about not telling the truth. Two days after Taylor had left town she called to tell Mom she was going to the music festival, and not to worry because Martin would look after her.

In total my sister was away from home for almost a fortnight, Martin dropped my sister home earlier today. I barely recognized Taylor because she looked really different. She had gotten a rose tattoo on her leg, and her hair was braided into long dreadlocks, I was impressed because I thought she looked like a real punk rocker. I expected my sister to be in big trouble. But our parents were mostly just relieved she was back home, Mom got upset when she saw my sister had a tattoo, and she was grounded for a month.

Later, Taylor came into my bedroom and we talked for a while.

"Thanks for not telling on me."

"It wasn't easy, I had to lie. I felt terrible—you shouldn't have asked me do that," I said.

"I'm sorry, Luke. You're right it wasn't fair."

"I want to go on my own adventures one day." I said.

"YOLO!" answered Taylor.

I listened as my sister described her travels — she talked about the different places she had visited, the buskers and pavement artists on the city streets, kind strangers, towering glass skyscrapers, and sleeping in hostels. She told me that seeing her favorite band perform live was one of the best moments of her life. I listened in awe of my sister's daring. The world suddenly seemed a far bigger place than I had ever imagined it to be.

The Moving Mountains

The crashing sound of big waves woke me up early on the morning of the regional surfing competition. It was too dark outside my bedroom window to see how big the waves were going to be. Over a breakfast of stacked pancakes with maple syrup, I watched a swell of stacked waves roll toward the beach.

"I don't know if I have the confidence to surf in those big waves," I confessed.

"Before you make up your mind just wait and see what happens. It's going to be the same for all the other contestants. You don't have to surf if you don't want to," said Dad. I knew I really didn't want to surf in the competition, but I also knew that someday I would have to confront my fear of surfing big waves.

Down at the competition, I gathered with the other surfers in my round, we each wore a different color shirt over our wetsuit so the judges could tell who was who out in the surf, and award our scores. I wore a blue shirt over my wetsuit.

Waiting on the beach before the huge waves with the other surfers, we made jokes about having to be saved if we wiped out, and we tried to stay focused on the challenge before us. When it came time to paddle out for my first round, I stood for a minute on the beach looking toward the hurtling walls of whitewater before me. I told myself: "Luke, you can make it out past those big waves!"

Paddling out through the surf, I thought about giving up and heading back to the beach. I doubted whether I was going to be able to make it out into the takeoff zone. The other surfers in my round were also struggling to make it out, but they hadn't given in, and I didn't want to be the first surfer to throw in the towel and quit.

I pushed my board under the waves in a duckdive motion; so they rolled right over the top of me, underwater I was being pushed and shoved by the powerful wave before I surfaced on the other side. Then I got my chance, the constant waves calmed for a couple of minutes between sets, and I paddled with all my strength. I made it out into the takeoff zone, where the waves first start to break; the other surfers in my round had also made it.

On my first big wave I slipped; the water launched me forward, but my feet slipped from my board when I jumped up. I fell headfirst from the top to the bottom of the wave. I took a deep breath of air right before the wave spun me upside-down underwater. I surfaced and gasped for air, I got back on my buoyant surfboard and continued paddling back towards the takeoff zone. I survived my first wipeout on a big wave.

"Luke, are you okay? I saw the whole wipeout it looked bad," one of the other surfers in my round asked.

"I hesitated for a minute then I slipped, the wave didn't hold me down for long, it wasn't too bad though," I replied.

In a strange way falling off eased my nerves; it was as though I had passed some invisible threshold that before I was afraid to cross.

Next I started riding the big waves without falling off; I won my first round, and my second and third rounds of the competition. I was on a roll and in tune with riding the waves, and by the afternoon I had made it into the final.

The other surfer in the final turned out to be my best friend Patrick. We had never come head-to-head like this in a big competition. Before the final, Mom said, "Luke, be careful out there. Those waves look dangerous."

"Mom, if something bad happens to me, promise you will look after Benson for me?" I said half-jokingly.

I didn't wait for her reply. I ran down onto the beach to join Patrick for our final. We shook hands on the beach.

"Good luck, Luke!" said Patrick,

"Whoever wins it doesn't matter, we will always be friends,"

"Yes, I agree let's just have fun and see who can ride the best wave!" replied Patrick.

I didn't have much strength left for paddling in my arms, but I made it out into the takeoff zone again. "Go, paddle for that wave," Patrick screamed. I turned toward the direction he was pointing and saw the wave he was pointing at. It was heading straight toward me and shaped like a moving mountain. I felt afraid, fear rose up in my chest, and then I had to decide what I was going to do. I thought: *Should I try and ride the biggest wave I have ever seen? Or should I let it go unridden?*

I didn't want all my friends and family to know that I was afraid to ride the big wave. Most of all I wanted to prove to myself: that I'm not a wimp!

There was no time for any self-doubt; the wave had already started to pull me into its vortex. I was committed to the takeoff whether I wanted to be or not, and I knew I really didn't want to fall on this monstrous wave.

I jumped to my feet and free fell for a second before my feet connected with my surfboard at the bottom of the wave. I had gotten past the most difficult part without falling, and it had taken all my skill and experience to not fall. I quickly turned up into the clean (unbroken) part of the large wave, as the heavy breaking lip arched behind me. The sound the crashing wave made was like the roar of a jet engine, and I could feel the immense power of water moving beneath my surfboard.

I stretched my arms out to balance on my surfboard; the wave was tall, at least double over my head, I had to choose my path for how I was going to navigate the rest of the ride. I decided to take a high line; surfing up high on the wave beneath the folding lip. I tried to speed forwards to avoid the monstrous white water that wanted to toss me off my surfboard.

I pumped my legs in rhythm with the fast moving wave. I was so busy trying not to fall or let the wave knock me off my board that I barely had time to do any turns that might help me to win the final. I was battling with the immense energy of the ocean instead.

Towards the end of my ride, the wave suddenly loomed up ready to closeout. A second before it finally collapsed I did a quick turn on my backhand, right underneath the breaking lip of the wave. I rode down with the lip and shot straight out in front as the wave exploded behind me into white water. My surfboard was pointed straight toward the beach, and I rode out victorious. I raised my arms above my head, to claim my ride, and I heard the crowd cheering on the beach. For the first time ever I felt like a real champion!

Right behind my wave, Patrick had caught his own massive wave but I only saw the end of his ride, and he surfed very well too! Then the bell rang which signaled the final was finished. I caught up with Patrick as we got out of the water.

"That was amazing, I just rode the best wave of my life," I said.

"We both caught massive waves and surfed well," said Patrick.

A crowd had gathered on the beach, my parents, my sister, and Benson were all there to congratulate me. I was pleased they had witnessed me riding the best wave of my life. Today was a special day. I knew I would never forget it!

"You surfed that wave like a professional surfer," my sister said.

"Thanks, it all happened so fast I didn't have time to think about what I was doing," I said.

In the evening at the prize giving ceremony we found out the results, and who had actually won the final.

The head judge announced the results. "First place, Patrick. Second place, Luke." I went up on stage with Patrick and I received a small silver trophy of a surfer standing on a wave. I was disappointed to find out I didn't win, but at least the person who had won was Patrick, and I was happy for him.

"Good final, Luke," said Patrick, as we shook hands after the awards ceremony.

"Congratulations, Patrick," I replied, trying not to let him see how disappointed I felt about getting second.

I was exhausted from surfing all day. On the drive home I asked, "Dad, who do you think should have won today? Me or Patrick?"

"It doesn't matter who won, you made it all the way to the final, you surfed that big wave, and that's all that matters," Dad said.

"But I really thought I should have won, Dad!"

"Well son, if counts so do I!"

When I got home I placed the small silver trophy of a surfer on top of my dresser; to remind me of the day I challenged my fear.

High School Blues

Major life update!

I switched high schools and moved away to study at boarding school in a different city. It wasn't an easy decision, but my parents convinced me it was in my best interest to attend a really good high school to improve my grades. The hardest part was that I would be far away from my dog, and my family and friends.

While I packed my suitcase, I decided to tell Benson the bad news; he seemed to sense that I was going away because he looked worried, and whined. I told my dog, "I'm going to be gone for at least one month, but I promise I'm coming back. You won't be able to find me even if you try, so please don't try. It's important that I go to a good high school. That's why I have to go." Benson looked at me with sadness in his eyes.

On my arrival at boarding school the first thing I did was take a tour. The campus was impressive; it had stone buildings with weird stone gargoyles, a tall old chapel, manicured lawns, a large wood paneled library with tomes of books, and spiraling staircases. I doubted that I could ever fit in at such a prestigious high school.

Next I met my new roommate, Andrew, he was an international student from South Korea. We both looked equally dismayed by the small size of our shared room for the semester. Andrew wore the thickest glasses I had ever seen. We traded stories about our homes. I told Andrew about how I was sad to leave my dog behind. Just talking about home made me feel homesick. Andrew gave me some sour-tasting fruit candy and a weird tasting, wrapped-up miniature sweet pineapple cake.

One thing I disliked right away about boarding school was the uniform; it was too formal. Preparing for the formal dinner, I had to wear a wool jacket, white shirt, gray pants and black leather shoes. The worst part was I had to wear a tie, and I didn't even know how to make a tie. It took me a dozen failed attempts in front of a mirror before I got it looking half-right. When classes started I found them really difficult, and all of my classmates were so smart, and I even failed my first chemistry test. I was so embarrassed. I wanted to return home right away during the first few weeks at boarding school.

Homework piled up every day. I spent every night studying. Fortunately, it turned out Andrew is a genius. He studied even later into the night than me and he knew the answer to all the math equations I got stuck on. He showed me how to work through the questions to find the right solution. I doubted if I could do it alone without his advice.

One afternoon I found my roommate sobbing. "What's wrong? Have a bad day?" I asked tentatively.

"I want to go home. Nobody likes me at this school," Andrew said between sobs. His glasses were all fogged up.

"That's not true. I'm just as homesick as you,"

"Well, you're my only friend then," Andrew said cheerfully.

After I talked with Andrew, I decided to call home. I told Mom about all the things I disliked about my high school: the uniforms, food, queues, and bullies. She told me I should give it more time, and it would get easier. I asked Mom about how Benson was doing without having me around. She said that he seemed to be doing fine.

Then she told me how she mistook Benson for a burglar. Apparently in the middle of the night Benson was banging on the back door with his paws, and standing upright on his back legs. Mom had crept toward the backdoor thinking it was a burglar. She could see the dark outline through the glass door, and she picked up a baseball bat just in case it. After a minute she realized it was only Benson knocking on the door in the darkness. I said, "Mom, Benson probably thought I was hiding from him at your house, and that's why he was knocking on the door. He wanted to find out if I was there or not!" I told her. I was pleased it wasn't a real burglar and that she didn't hit Benson with a baseball bat by accident.

I found it hard not being able to go out surfing while at boarding school. Being away from the waves made me feel like I was missing out on so many good days of surfing. I daydreamed about surfing during boring classes. Skateboarding soon became my substitute for not being able to surf. I made friends with a group of classmates who liked to skateboard. We hung out together once classes were finished. We jumped over steps on our skateboards, doing kick flips. The only problem was that skateboarding was forbidden on campus, so if a teacher saw us we had to speed away fast on our skateboards.

I didn't know playing music was so popular amongst teenagers until I joined the music club at my new high school. I tried to practice at least everyday, and I really improved playing the saxophone. I don't get frustrated when I make small mistakes, like when I first started learning.

During lunch break one day, I heard a commotion going on between two students. I went to see what was happening. It was between Tucker (a bully), and my roommate Andrew. Tucker was shoving Andrew and he fell to his knees and scrambled to find his glasses. Seeing that Andrew was in trouble I stepped forward to try and intervene. I had to help my roommate.

"Leave Andrew alone! He did nothing wrong," I said to Tucker, the high school bully. Tucker swung around toward me as I spoke.

"What did you say, loser?"

"I said leave him alone," I repeated.

"I'm really scared what are you going to do? Karate kick me," remarked the bully. Some of the schoolboys who had gathered around laughed. Andrew got back up and I motioned for him to leave and he hurried away in the opposite direction.

Tucker pushed me in the chest, and I shoved him right back, we tussled one another for a minute. Then I pushed him again and he stumbled backward. I knew I had to stand up for myself. Tucker looked stunned then he rushed toward me a second time. I saw his punch coming a second too late. His knuckles glanced my nose. I had managed to avoid the worst of it by stepping backward, but my nose still gushed with blood, staining my gray school shirt.

The gathered crowd of schoolboys pushed us apart, and the fight was finished. After our fight, Tucker and I were called to have a meeting with the headmaster. Tucker and I avoided one another's angry gaze and kept our heads lowered as we waited outside his office. My nose had swollen up.

"Come into my office," said the headmaster, and we walked into the large wood-paneled room. We sat in the two seats in front of the long wooden desk behind which the headmaster glared at us.

"I understand the two of you had a fight," said the headmaster.

"Yes, sir," we both answered at the same time.

"I'm not interested in hearing your excuses for who caused the fight, but let me say this: fighting is not tolerated at this school, if you want to remain a student here you better stop. You're both suspended for one week, and you will be sent home." I only listened to one magical word: HOME!

The next evening, I looked out of an airplane window, it was dark and rain was streaming down the window. The ride had been turbulent ever since we took off, and the small plane was shaking so hard. I had never flown in such bad weather. I glimpsed briefly in the darkness below some faint lights sparkling, which I knew was my hometown. I knew my parents would be waiting at the airport, and Benson would be waiting at home. I had been away at high school for almost six weeks and it seemed like my old life was far away.

The plane made a bumpy landing. I was pleased to have my feet firmly on the ground again as I walked towards the airport arrivals gate, I caught sight of my parents waiting together for me inside, and I smiled at seeing them again, I was worried how they were going to react the news of my suspension.

"Oh, Luke. I was so worried about you flying in such terrible weather," Mom said.

"Welcome home. Looks like he got you a good one," said Dad, he pointed at my swollen nose.

"It wasn't my fault, I promise. I was just defending my roommate. I would never start a fight for no reason." I remarked.

"Sometimes boys fight. I know I had my fights when I was your age, but that doesn't make it okay," Dad said.

"I don't want this to happen ever again. Do you understand?" asked Mom.

"Yes, I'm really sorry I promise it won't happen again," I said.

When I arrived home, Benson was already waiting at the gate at Dad's house. That's were he stayed while I was away at boarding school. He spotted me as soon as our truck pulled into the driveway. His tail was swinging from side to side as I stepped out of the truck. He raced toward me and when he was a yard away he jumped up and placed his two giant paws on my shoulders, standing upright with just his hind legs. He gave me a bear hug. Benson stood as tall as me and he had grown even bigger since I had been away. I said, "I told you I would return, but it's only for a short visit before I have to go back to boarding school. We're just going to have to get used to me coming and going from now on."

Star Striker

For some reason I ended up on the worst soccer team for the whole season.

Back at boarding school for another term, I decided to try out for the soccer trials. I had to choose a sport to play anyway and soccer seemed a good fit.

Kicking a soccer ball around wasn't too difficult, but I didn't have much experience playing soccer compared to some of my teammates who had been playing for years.

During my first trial game, I did my best to impress the head coach who was selecting players for the different teams. I even had a shot at the goal but missed. I thought I had done well during the trial, well enough to make a top team. As I waited in a line with the other boys who had played in the trial game, the coach selecting the "A" team called out the names of the players who had made the top team. I didn't get my name called out, and I felt really disappointed. Afterward, I went to talk with the coach.

"I don't understand why I didn't make the team, coach? I've always been good at sport," I said.

"Luke, you played quite well in the trial game, but you don't seem to understand all the rules of the game. There's always next season." The coach shrugged his shoulders and walked away.

One week later I had my first training session with my new teammates, and I discovered our team didn't even have a coach! So we just ran around kicking the ball between one another, and when it came to kicking goals I scored every time I had a shot. Our team was a mixed bunch of players; some had more skills than others, and just a few players were better at soccer than me.

John became our unofficial coach and team captain. He was the best soccer player on the team, the only reason he was looked over for the "A" team was because he was too short. He took control of our training sessions without anyone ever really asking him to. He was a natural team leader. I got along well with John and he gave me tips on how to improve my goal kicking.

At the end of our first practice, we had to decide what positions we were going to play for our upcoming game on the weekend. There were some arguments about who should be playing where, and I wasn't sure about what position I should play because it was my first season playing soccer, because in the past the only sport I did was surfing.

"Luke, you're good at shooting goals. You can be a striker," John announced to the team.

I was pleased to be a striker for our team. It seemed to be one of the most important positions; my main role was to score the goals. After training was finished, I thought:

Maybe I was meant to be on this team, I doubt I would have been a striker if I had made it into the 'A' team.

On the weekend I had to borrow a spare pair of soccer boots for the first game because I hadn't managed to buy my own pair in time. I had used my jogging shoes for the trials.

"You can keep them. They're my old pair from last season," John said, as he threw the black and white soccer boots at my feet.

"Thanks, I'm ready to score some goals now," I said.

Getting ready for the game, I jogged around the field with my teammates. We were all wearing our blue soccer shirts with black shorts. Our opponents from another school were all dressed in red soccer shirts. My new soccer boots pinched my toes as I warmed up, because they were one size too small.

During the game I got to take a corner kick.

"Try and get the ball to where Eric is," John whispered in my ear as I lined up the soccer ball. I could see Eric shuffling around some defenders in the square close by the goal.

"Okay, I'll try my best shot," I said.

Then the referee blew the whistle. I kicked the ball with just the tip of my toe striking the bottom of the ball. It spun up into the blue sky. It arched over players' heads towards Eric but the ball didn't go exactly where I wanted it to, and instead it passed over Eric and landed out of play. I had blown my first chance at crossing the ball for a goal.

"I blew that one," I said disappointed.

"Don't blow your next chance, Luke. We need to score at least one goal to win, and the whole team is counting on you," said John.

"I will do better next time!"

While I ran back to my position on the field, I knew I wouldn't blow it if I got a second chance at scoring a goal.

The game stopped for the half time break. The game was still scoreless. Our team huddled together and John instructed us with some urgency, he said, "Right now everyone is playing for himself, we need to play like a team, so if you get the ball pass it to our strikers."

My second chance came shortly after the break, it was the moment I had been waiting for all game. John, who plays midfield, managed to cross the ball to me. His cross was in front of me and I had to chase after the ball to reach it before a defender got to it first. With the ball safely between my running feet, I dodged the first defender, then a second defender, and a third. I saw the goal open up in front of me, and the goalies waving arms. He shouted something. I kicked the ball with full force. It soared straight up into the blue sky and toward the space behind the goalie's left shoulder exactly where I had wanted it to go. The goalie dived toward the flying soccer ball but he missed. The soccer ball swung into the back of the goal where it got caught up in the net.

Some of the parents of my teammates started cheering from the sidelines; for a second I felt sad that my own parents weren't there to see it. The referee blew his whistle for a goal, and my teammates ran up and hugged me.

"I knew you were going to make a great striker!" John said.

"Awesome kick," Eric congratulated me.

It had all happened so fast, a blur of dodging defenders, green grass, and the ball flying towards the net like magic. I doubted whether I could kick such a perfect goal again.

That's how we won our first soccer game of the season, 1-0

Sweet Sixteen

The best part of turning sixteen is being (legally) old enough to drive. On the day of my sixteenth birthday my parents agreed to buy me a car. We went shopping together to a secondhand car dealership. Picking a car wasn't an easy decision, at least not on my budget. But I found the perfect car: a red Honda. My car has a few dents and worn upholstery, but to me it could have been a Corvette.

"Thanks, a car is the best birthday present ever!" I said.

"It's up to you to pay for the gas," remarked Mom.

"No speeding. I don't want you driving above sixty mph, okay?" said Dad.

"No problem. I won't speed I promise!"

I started working on building sites for Dad during the school holidays so I can afford to pay for my own gas.

A car is the ultimate milestone for a teenager. I no longer have to wait around for rides, or catch the bus when I want to go into the city.

Patrick also recently got, a Jeep. During the weekends we often drove out to an old abandoned quarry on the outskirts of town, popular with teenagers. It is a safe place to spin rubber over loose gravel tracks and plunge through giant mud puddles while also improving our driving skills.

Whenever I'm about to go in my car somewhere, Benson had a special ability for knowing in advance. By the time I walk out the door and head down the driveway, Benson was already sitting beside my car with a pleading look as if to ask, "Can I come for a ride with you?" I usually bring Benson along when I drive somewhere. He filled up the entire back seat, and his favorite thing to do was stick his head out the window while I was speeding down the highway at fifty-five mph. His hair gets blown about, his ears flap in the wind, he sniffed all the smells of the countryside, and his pink tongue was flying halfway out his mouth. I guessed my dog liked driving in the quick lane even more than I do. If it was up to Benson I think he would like it if we just kept driving on the highway without ever stopping.

The only time I leave Benson behind was when I went to visit my new girlfriend, Melissa. We met each other at a party a couple of months ago. It wasn't long before we exchanged numbers and had started officially dating.

I didn't even think about Charlotte anymore. I try and visit her at least twice a week. We watch comedy movies with popcorn, and walk around downtown or just hang out in coffee shops. Melissa was my first (serious) girlfriend. I have even been out for dinner with her family to a fancy Thai restaurant.

I had a birthday party and invited all of my friends and family. We drank soda from red Solo cups while Dad grilled up a feast on the barbecue. Taylor was at my party with Martin, her long-term boyfriend. After all this time I was surprised they were still together, I was wrong about my first impression of Martin not being reliable.

Benson walked about greeting everyone at my party, my dog was older too! Recently I had noticed he wasn't as fast running along the beach anymore, and slept longer during the day.

When it came to blowing out the sparkling candles on the birthday cake cut out in the shape of the number seventeen which Mom had made, I made a wish. Towards the end of my party, I gave an impromptu short jazz performance with my saxophone, as I played for all of my guests, Benson joined in with a loud howl.

Squirrel Trouble

I'm spending another summer vacation at the lake house.
Earlier today Benson decided to get into a whole lot of trouble;
and I had a front row seat to watch it all play out.

I was sunbathing on the lakeshore when I caught sight
of Benson, running along the narrow path up along the top
of the rocky cove cliff that lead to a lookout over the lake. He
was chasing a squirrel, and the squirrel lead Benson right to
the cliff edge. The squirrel vanished up a tree growing nearby,
while Benson blindly ran off the cliff edge.

I could see the bad situation my dog was in and I knew
I had to do something to help him. Benson was stuck a few
yards from the top. A small shrub had stopped him from falling
the whole way down the vertical cliff (a drop of approximately
twenty-five feet) onto jagged rocks below on the lakeshore. I
could see how terrified Benson was as he struggled to hold
his position; trying not to slip any further, and I was afraid of
what might happen next.

"Hang on Benson, I'm coming to rescue you!" I yelled.

Some of the different ideas I had for how I might be able
to save my dogs life, I ran through my mind. It was a desper-
ate situation. At first it seemed as though there was nothing I
could do to stop the worst from happening. If Benson slipped

any further from where he was; I doubted he would survive the fall, and I had to push such terrible thoughts aside if I was going to be any help to him. Benson and I were alone. There was nobody around close by to help. Everyone else had gone over to the general store on the other side of the lake. I screamed out anyway, "Help, help! Please, somebody come and help!" But it was no use.

I had two different ideas for saving Benson. The first idea was that I could find something to place beneath him to break his fall. The second was I could try and rescue him from above on the cliff edge.

"I'm coming back Benson, please just don't give up!" I shouted up to Benson. I had tears streaming down my face. I started running in the direction of the boatshed. It tore my heart to leave Benson alone not knowing if he would still be there when I got back.

I ran so fast my lungs were hurting. I knew every second mattered. When I reached the boathouse I pulled the sliding doors open; I was lucky the boathouse was unlocked. Inside I searched around the two large sailing yachts. It didn't take me more than thirty seconds to find what I needed.

The rope was sitting on the bow of the smallest yellow sailing yacht. It was looped in a figure eight pattern. I quickly grabbed the rope and inspected it. The rope looked strong enough to hold Benson, but I didn't know if it was the right length for what I was planning to use it for. I thought: *Perhaps I can save Benson after all*. I ran back towards the path that leads to a lookout over the lake, where Benson had slipped.

When I reached the cliff edge, I was careful not to slip myself as I peered down to look at Benson. I felt nauseous from the heights. I could see Benson a few yards below me; but he was out of reach and it was too dangerous for me to climb down to him. "I'm up here now Benson. Don't worry; I have a plan to rescue you. But we have to work together, okay?" I said. Benson turned his head and looked up at me with relief in his eyes.

Patrick had taught me a knot when we went rock climbing together. I quickly threaded the rope through my fingers. I put one end of the rope through a circle and I made a lasso with the rope. I wasn't sure if it was going to work the way I wanted it to but it was our best chance.

I estimated about three long minutes had passed since Benson had first slipped. I could tell time was starting to run out because I wasn't sure how much longer Benson could hold his precarious position. Small rocks were beginning to give way under his paws, and I heard them crash on the rocks below.

Next I took aim at Benson and threw the lasso down over the rock edge. It missed him, so I tried a second time. The rope spun through the air with deadly accuracy it landed right over Benson's nose and settled over his head, just like I had hoped it would. But I still needed to get the rope around his chest.

"Wave your paw, Benson!" I called out the command I had taught him for the dog show. Benson remembered the command, and he lifted his right paw. At the same time I tugged on the rope gently so that his paw went through the loop of the lasso. "Wave your left paw, now," I instructed, and he did the same with his left paw. I tugged on the rope again so that it pulled past his neck, and settled over his front legs, and safely around his chest. "Nice job, that's perfect, now just hang!" I said.

With the rope in place, I breathed a sign of relief I knew the worst was over and that my plan should work, but I still had to lower Benson all the way down the cliff face to the bottom, because he was too heavy for me to pull up to the top.

A moment later and without warning the small shrub that had stopped Benson falling gave way beneath him. The shrub tumbled towards the rocks, and I felt the full weight of Benson on the other end of the rope. I was holding onto the fate of my big dog.

I held on with all my strength, I knew how much depended on hanging on. I slowly started to release the rope in my fingers a few centimeters at a time, the rope held firm around Benson's chest, as I lowered him down centimeter by centimeter, he was swinging in the air with nothing beneath him. It reminded me of the time I had lost my grip while rock climbing and the safety rope had saved me, and Patrick had given me a hand up.

I let go of more and more of the rope. It was starting to run out of length. I knew I couldn't let go of the rope because Benson was relying on me and I had to bear the pain as the muscles in my arms started to ache.

As I lowered almost all of the remaining rope, Benson disappeared from my view. I knew he must be close to reaching the ground but I wasn't sure. As I released the last couple of yards of the rope, I felt the strain go off the rope release, and that's when I heard Benson bark.

I let go of the rope and ran back down the path back towards the lakeshore below, to check that he had made it down without injury.

Benson was standing at the bottom on a flat rock next to the lakeshore. The rope was still tangled around his chest. I was pleased to see that he didn't look injured. He was excited to greet me as I untied the rope that had saved him.

"That was a really close call, I was so worried you might not survive this mistake, please don't scare me like that ever again!" I said. Benson was shaking from shock. I petted him to calm him down. I could see in his eyes how happy he was to be safely down from where he fell. "You shouldn't have chased that squirrel over the cliff edge like that. What were you thinking? You're smarter than that."

But I was too exhausted to be angry about the situation; I knew mistakes could happen to anyone, I do stupid things all the time, but this was by far the worst mistake of my dog's life.

Later, as Benson slept on the porch the events from earlier flashed through my mind like a movie. Everything had unfolded so quickly, as though it wasn't real, and I knew that today my dog had dodged a bullet.

I was pleased that I had been able to save Benson when he really needed help. Somebody had looked out for us today.

Future Self

Senior year has been keeping me busy between soccer practice, saxophone rehearsals, socializing and studying. So I haven't had time to write in here.

Earlier Andrew and I played Minecraft after our classes were over. Then we started talking about the future and I realized that I didn't yet have much of a plan. Andrew already wanted to become a medical scientist, so he can help find a cure for cancer.

"I think you're smart enough to be a brilliant medical scientist," I said.

"What do you want to do, Luke?"

"I haven't really given it too much thought. When I was younger I wanted to be a professional surfer. But it doesn't really seem realistic anymore,"

Andrew seemed surprised by my naive answer. "Luke, don't you think you should make a plan for your career? High school will be finished at the end of the year, and soon you will need to apply for college. You're going to college aren't you?"

"I don't know if I will go to college, but how did you figure out that you want to become a medical scientist?" I asked.

"Well, I've always liked science and medicine. I think it will be easier for you to make a decision when you select a subject you like and are good at."

"I will never be as smart as you. I don't think I could ever become a medical scientist because I suck at math and science," I said.

"Luke, you should have more confidence in yourself! You're better at different subjects than me. You play the saxophone well, and you're athletic too. I'm hopeless at sport. Maybe you should study music?"

"I guess you're right. Deciding what career to follow is the biggest puzzle for a teenager," I answered.

After my conversation with Andrew, I realized that I didn't want my career to be a surprise.

The Big Orchestra

Music has been taking up a big part of my time recently.

Every year the graduating music class played an orchestra concert at high school. I shuffled about onstage trying to find my spot, but there was barely any room to spare.

There was a audience of at least 200 people seated in the big music hall. Onstage were around thirty of my classmates with a whole ensemble of different instruments (cello, violin, harp, bass, trumpet, drums, piano and saxophone).

The conductor stood before us, the lights dimmed, the conductor pointed his baton at a group of assembled musicians, and the concert had started.

The sound of a big orchestra playing is hard to describe, but the noise of all the assembled different instruments playing together, the symphony a combination of rich high and low notes that rise up in a crescendo, like a rising wave. The noise made the hair on my arms, and the back of my neck stick up.

While I waited for my turn to play my part, I was nervous and I kept my eyes fixed on the sheets of music in front of me even though I knew all the music anyway. I thought back to when I first started learning how to play the saxophone, when I had wanted to quit right away, and when my only audience was Benson falling asleep as he listened to me practice in my bedroom. I realized how much progress I had made so far with my music. I had come along way since then. I deserved to be onstage and I wanted to enjoy the night, my first big orchestra, and I relaxed a little more as I stood in front of the big audience. Tonight was my big moment to show how far I had come at playing the saxophone.

Suddenly the conductor spun around ninety degrees. I saw his shoulders begin to move first, then I caught his eyes full of expectation, he pointed his baton straight at me. It was my turn to play. I breathed in deeply, my fingers instinctually found the right dials, my mind became focused, and I blew through my saxophone with the correct timing to keep the music flowing.

After the orchestra was finished all my classmates gathered backstage, everyone was pleased with how well our first big orchestra performance had gone. I didn't know when I would next see my classmates again, because tonight marked a turning point: high school would be finished forever by the end of the week.

Finals

The finals' schedule was printed out on a poster board in the hallway at high school; after finding the right room, I waited in the crowded hallway for my final exam to begin.

"Good luck, Luke," Andrew said.

"Thanks, I know you will ace finals," I answered.

I had studied hard to be ready for finals, and I was ready to get started. A bell rang and students started filing out from the basketball hall, the room where our finals were being held. At least a hundred shuffling students entered the hall, long lines of desks were lined up in tidy rows. I found a desk and sat down and then I saw the exam paper was already waiting facedown on the table in front of me.

The exam administrator announced, "You have five minutes reading time, then you can begin to write your answers. In total you will have one hour to complete the paper."

After flipping the paper over, I browsed through all the questions. Some of the questions looked difficult to answer hard, and some I knew I could answer correctly. The reading time elapsed and I picked up my pencil to begin writing. I decided to start with the easier questions first.

When I reached the end of the paper, I looked up and discovered I was one of the last students still seated on the huge basketball hall, it was like I had been in a time warp, because I did not even notice everyone leaving before me; but I was okay with being one of the last to finish.

After handing in my paper to the administrator, I smiled and rushed out into the hallway. I caught sight of a bunch of my classmates still hanging around.

"How did you find the exam, Luke?" one classmate asked.

"I don't really know. I think some of the questions were OK, but I got stuck on a few problems too. How did you find it?"

"It wasn't bad, I thought the exam was easy, that's why so many people finished early."

"I guess it wasn't so bad!" I agreed.

We walked towards the exit as the late afternoon sunlight lite up the hallway before us and shone brightly in our eyes.

For the graduation ceremony a few weeks later, my classmates and I, all wore a green-apple silk gowns, with a green cap. I shuffled next to my fellow students as we got closer and closer to the stage. I watched as my friends graduated before me, and I knew it would be my turn in just a minute. I looked into the sea of the crowded auditorium. I spotted Taylor and Mom seated toward the front and toward the back of the hall I caught sight of Dad. My parents were still separated. "Luke Fine," I felt dizzy as I heard my name called out. I walked forward onto stage to accept my certificate from the principal.

"Congratulations, Luke. I wish you all the best for your future," said the principal,

"Thanks!" I replied.

He shook my hand; a camera flashed in my eyes, and in an instant high school was over.

Following graduation I checked the mailbox daily waiting for acceptance letters from the colleges I had applied to study at.

"Luke, a letter has arrived for you, it looks official," said Mom. I burst out of my room and toward the unopened letter waiting on the kitchen table. I examined the thick cream envelope. I recognized the red emblem printed on the top corner. It was from a prestigious college, the one I really hoped to gain admission to, more than any of the others.

"Go on, open it!" Mom said. I opened the letter, it read:

> *Dear Luke Fine,*
>
> *Thank you for applying to study at Harvey University. On behalf of the Admissions Committee, we are pleased to offer you admission to study in the School of Music. You should be proud of your achievement.*
>
> *Congratulations.*
>
> *Sincerely,*
> *Director of Admissions, Harvey University.*

Reading the letter out loud, I could hardly believe I had gotten accepted to such an excellent college. The letter was like a key that seemed to suddenly unlock my future. I laughed loudly. I jumped up and down, and yelled out: "I got accepted to Harvey University!"

"I don't believe you. Let me see the letter," Mom said as she snatched the letter away from me.

"I'm so proud of you, Luke. You've worked so hard for this. Just wait until your Dad hears the good news."

Benson heard Mom and I celebrating and he ran inside. I told him the good news, "I got accepted, Benson!"

He jumped up and placed his paws on my shoulders, just like he had done before, all those years ago when I first arrived home from boarding school.

Scary Thunderstorm

I went to visit my grandparents who lived downtown. Grandpa needed help whitewashing a new fence so I drove over and I brought Benson along with me. I worked painting all the afternoon and I decided to stay over for the night, to finish the last of the painting in the morning. I didn't think Benson would mind sleeping on the back porch for the night.

I heard the noise first, I was asleep but the noise woke me up, the cracking sound of a thunderstorm. I looked at my watch and it was almost midnight. I quickly jumped out of bed in my pajamas and ran to check that Benson was okay, because I knew how much he dislikes thunderstorms. But he wasn't in the backyard where I had left him. I could see the fence was slightly damaged in one place and I guessed that Benson must have jumped over the fence.

After I ran back inside, I got changed as fast as possible. I pulled on my jeans, T-shirt, and brown leather jacket. Grandpa came into the room. "Is everything okay, Luke? I heard you crashing about," he asked.

"No, everything isn't okay! It's Benson. He's not in the yard. He must have gotten out of the backyard. He doesn't like loud noises and the thunderstorm must have scared him. We have to hurry, I have to find him!"

"Well, let me get my jacket," said Grandpa.

"We can take my car. It's already in the driveway," I said, as I grabbed my keys.

The weather had worsened without any warning, and white flashes of lightning illuminated the suburbs for intervals of a few seconds at a time as I drove around the suburb looking for Benson.

At one point I thought I glimpsed the illuminated, outline of a running dog. I stopped the car, ran out into the pouring rain and called out, "Benson, come here, boy! It's me, Luke," I screamed, but my voice was lost in the whipping crackle, and gunshot boom of loud thunder above me. I shuddered and I was afraid of the raging thunderstorm, and I understood then why Benson was afraid of loud noises.

Grandpa stuck his fingers in his mouth and whistled loudly but nothing happened. I thought my mind had played a trick on me and the running dog I had seen was just an illusion. The rain got worse. We headed back into my car to continue searching.

He told me, "Drive toward the highway, Luke. Maybe Benson headed toward all the moving lights."

When we reached the edge of the highway. I saw all the car lights snaked past us at speed. Looking at the highway I was filled with dread and I hoped Benson didn't run in this direction. He would be in real danger here with all the moving cars.

Our search turned up no sign of my dog. All our calls had gone unanswered. We headed back to Grandpa's townhouse to go back to sleep. We were going to have to continue the search in the early morning. Before I went to sleep I said a short prayer for Benson that he may be safe. I had trouble getting back to sleep. I couldn't help but feel it was my entire fault, I should have left him at home then none of this would have happened.

In the morning I continued my search for Benson because he still hadn't returned. Soon my entire family started searching for my dog, I even made a flyer with a picture of Benson on it with my cell phone number, which I placed around the suburbs surrounding my grandparents' townhouse. I even drove around the city back alleys looking behind Dumpsters. Soon days passed without Benson anywhere in sight.

After another day had passed without Benson showing up, I started to fear the worst had happened, and that I wasn't going to see my Bernese mountain dog ever again.

My Mom told me not to give up and that there was still a chance he was alive. I had a strange feeling deep down that my dog was OK. I made a pact with myself not to ever give up looking for Benson. Mom also thought that if Benson was still alive he might find his way all the way back home from the city.

"Dogs have a knack for following their nose, and finding their way home," she said.

"I hope he does because I really miss my dog, Mom," I said.

That evening, I put some spaghetti and meatballs (Benson's favorite dinner) in his silver dog bowl by the backdoor just in case he followed his nose back to his family.

First Snow Fall

A different storm blew into town today. I watched the line of dark clouds roll in from a distance. I thought about where Benson was in the bad weather, he had been missing for six nights. Then heavy snowflakes started to drift sideways down toward the ground and after a couple of hours the whole front yard was covered with white snow, even the top of Benson's kennel. I don't remember the last time it snowed like this where I lived.

I decided to make a Snowman in the front yard and while I was outside I saw something moving on the road. Despite the poor visibility I recognized Benson right away. I raced toward him, slipping and sliding across the snow to get to him as soon as possible.

A Bernese mountain dog is made for the snow, and Benson made an impressive outline with his black, white and brown coat against the snowy landscape. He was walking slowly with a slight limp. He looked tired and thinner than normal.

Benson did not see that I was racing toward him at first. His eyes were fixed on the snow in front of him. "Benson, Benson . . . Benson!" I called out, and then he looked up suddenly. He walked slowly but when he saw me he jumped toward me with his tail wagging.

I couldn't believe my eyes. I was happy to see that my dog was alive, and I gave him a hug.

"Do you know how worried I was? I searched everywhere trying to find you. I didn't give up looking for you, I promise." I explained, I could see the relief in his eyes.

I brought Benson into the house to warm him up. I grabbed dry towels, placed dog food in his bowl and gave him water to drink. He drank all the water, but only ate half the dog food. I thought that was strange because Benson usually has a mighty appetite. My dog walked into the lounge, stretched his big paws out in front of the fire and fell asleep straight away.

Throughout the afternoon Benson had a steady stream of visitors: the whole neighborhood had helped me look for my dog, and people came to pay a visit once they heard he was home. But Benson was too tired to get up and he just watched all his friends from where he lay.

I drove Benson to the veterinary clinic because he had a bad cough. It was raining cats and dogs the whole drive. The vet did some tests, he even took an x-ray, but he warned me that Benson was unwell and that his condition might not improve. The vet prescribed some medicine to help with his cough. Driving home I felt sad by what the vet had told me. I didn't want Benson to know how I was feeling, so I acted cheerfully.

A few weeks passed, Benson still had a rasping cough; he didn't seem to be getting over it. I took Benson down to the beach and we played together as though nothing had changed between us over all this time.

Later in the evening Benson's condition got worse. My dog seemed to have trouble breathing, his breathes were irregular, his nose started to run. I lay beside him in the lounge, and our family gathered around. I talked to Benson about all our adventures.

"I'm sure you haven't forgotten about the time I saved you with a lasso when you ran off the cliff at the lake? What about when we won the show dog competition? What about when you carried a log the size of a tree on the beach? Or when you hid under Moms house for almost a week?" I said.

Benson watched me as I spoke. His eyes were alert, and he whacked my leg with his tail occasionally as if to say, "Yes! Of course I remember. How could I ever forget these events?" So I knew he still remembered everything.

I decided to go to bed at eleven p.m. "Goodnight, Benson. I will see you in the morning," I whispered in his ear. I'm not sure if he heard me because he had already closed his eyes. At first I couldn't sleep because I could hear Benson breathing loudly from the lounge, and then outside the wind rattled against the trees. It started to rain softly at first, and then it grew to become a loud downpour and I drifted off to sleep.

When I woke up I sensed that something was wrong. The house was too quiet. I walked out of bed and down the corridor toward the lounge. That's when I saw Benson: he was lying in the same position from last night, he looked like he was peacefully asleep, but as I got closer I realized he wasn't breathing. I reached out and tried to shake him, but nothing happened. He felt cold. "Benson, wake up!" I cried, tears fell from my eyes; I collapsed on the ground next to him and wrapped my arms around his shoulders.

Taylor rushed into the lounge. "What's happened to Benson, Luke? Tell me he's okay?" she asked.

"I found him lying like this when I woke up. There's not another dog like Benson in the whole world."

"Oh, no! Luke, I'm so sorry. Benson was special to all of us," my sister said.

Benson, my dog who had been my best friend, had passed away. I never thought this sad day would come.

Later my family gathered around for the sendoff, we buried my dog at sunset, up on a hill overlooking the sea and his favorite beach. I said a few heartfelt final words, "You were the best Bernese mountain dog a boy could have ever asked for. You had a special way of getting into trouble, but together we always managed to overcome the obstacles. You had a big heart and brought us all closer together, and you always gave 100% effort to everything you did. Goodbye, Benson."

I planted a small oak tree sapling close by. I could tell one day it would grow into a big oak tree.

College Bound

I'm now nineteen!

Without my dog it felt like a huge chasm had opened up in my life. I tried not to think about how much I missed him, especially when I go out surfing and he was not chasing along beside me on the beach. Things are just different without Benson around.

A strange thing happened one week ago as I walked to college for my first day. I saw a Bernese mountain dog on the bustling city sidewalk. I made eye contact with the dog and as it walked toward me the dog wore a big grin, had friendly eyes, and his tail whacked the side of my leg as we passed one another. Seeing that Bernese mountain dog instantly made me think of Benson; all the good memories I had shared with my dog raced back to me, I laughed because I could tell that Benson was looking down on me for this special day.

Seven years had sped by since I worked my first jobs and saved five hundred dollars so I could afford my very own Bernese mountain dog. I doubt anyone would believe all the stories I have written in this diary about my dog were true.

THE END

To Discover More Books & Entertainment Visit:

http://lemonade.money/

Note

About the Author

The Boy Who Got A Bernese Mountain is the debut by Brook Ardon.

*Please leave a review on Amazon and follow my author page for updates.

Note

Left Blank

Made in the USA
Lexington, KY
21 September 2018